T. J. Folger, Thief

by *Steven Kroll*

illustrated by *Bill Morrison*

Holiday House, New York

Library of Congress Cataloging in Publication Data

Kroll, Steven.
T. J. Folger, thief.

SUMMARY: T. J. Folger brags he is the greatest
thief in the world until a mystery thief teaches
him a lesson.
[1. Robbers and outlaws—Fiction] I. Morrison,
Bill. II. Title.
PZ7.K9225Tac   [Fic]   77-24575
ISBN 0-8234-0313-0

FOR WALKER COWEN,
who kept me at it

The Jacket

T.J. Folger loved his jacket. He wore it everywhere. He wore it to school every day. He wore it on trips. He wore it to the park. Sometimes he wore it to the dinner table. Sometimes he even wore it to bed.

The jacket was long and flappy. It had two big pockets on the top, and two big pockets on the bottom. It had a zipper pocket on the inside and a lining with an open seam. The right sleeve had a hole for candy bars or a pocket knife. T.J. Folger was a thief, and the jacket was part of his act.

The School Bus

Getting on the school bus, T.J. Folger noticed the comb sticking out of Tom the driver's back pocket. T.J. took the comb. It fit neatly into the hole in his sleeve. Tom pulled the bus away from the curb and drove on. T.J. sat down next to Mike in the back of the bus.

The bus stopped again. Alice and Freddy got on just as T.J. pocketed Mike's ruler.

No one noticed a thing.

The Classroom

T.J. was the first one in his classroom. He looked out the door to see if anyone was coming. No one was, not even Mr. Peck, the teacher.

Quickly T.J. opened Pamela's desk, then Donald's, then Roger's. He took a tube of glue, a yellow pad, and a little china dog. He put them all under some papers in his own desk.

Then he went back for some of Georgia Peck's rubber bands.

Just as he was grabbing a handful, Mr. Peck walked in.

"T.J.," said Mr. Peck, "what are you doing at my daughter's desk?"

"Oh, hi," said T.J., smiling broadly. "I was just returning some of Georgia's rubber bands."

He replaced the rubber bands and closed the desk. He went back to his chair and sat down. The other kids arrived and took their seats. Mr. Peck began taking attendance.

No one had noticed a thing.

Recess

At recess the kids went to play ball, swing on the swings, or slide on the slides.

T.J. Folger wasn't very athletic. He never got a hit, and swinging on the swings scared him. He stood around bragging instead.

"You know what?" said T.J.

"What?" said Pamela.

"I'm the greatest thief in the world."

"Oh, yeah?" said Pamela. "Says who?"

T.J. puffed out his chest. "You name it. I can steal it."

"Go steal the flagpole then."

T.J. looked at the giant flagpole standing in the middle of the school yard.

"Well, maybe not the flagpole," he said.

The Candy Store

After school T.J. went straight to the candy store on the corner. He edged in through the door. He edged up to the candy counter.

Old Mr. Herman, the owner, was busy fixing a customer a milk shake. A couple of other kids were standing around looking at the candy.

T.J. slipped an Oh Henry! into the hole in his sleeve. He stuck some Chuckles into the upper right-hand pocket of his jacket. A Spiderman comic fit in the open seam. Then he went and paid for a Hershey bar.

Mr. Herman accepted the money. T.J. turned to go. "Wait!" said Mr. Herman. "Wait one moment, please!"

T.J. froze. He would go to jail. His parents would hate him. Everyone in school would make fun of him.

Mr. Herman came up beside him. Should he try to run? Mr. Herman placed three pennies in his hand. "You forgot your change," he said.

Home

At home T.J. dumped his loot on the bed. The comb was old and missing a few teeth. He threw it in the wastebasket. The ruler fit neatly into the drawer of his bedside table. The candy bars went under his mattress. The comic went on a shelf with three hundred and forty-two others. The other stuff he'd left in his desk at school.

T.J. sighed. Everything taken care of. No evidence in evidence. Then he ambled down the hall to his father's study.

"Hi, Dad," said T.J. in the doorway.

"Hello, son. Could you come back later? I've got to finish typing this chapter."

"Okay," said T.J. He walked away. He walked as far as the hall table. There on the table was his father's wallet.

T.J. slipped a five-dollar bill out of the

wallet. He replaced the wallet in exactly the
same spot.

No one would notice a thing.

The Chopper

T.J. Folger went to the park. In the park he liked to play cops and robbers with the other kids. He liked to be one of the bad guys. He'd run far away and hide in a tree. No one would ever find him. No one was ever pleased about that.

The only people in the park this afternoon were a boy and his mother. They were sitting together on a bench. The boy's shiny, five-speed chopper was leaning against a tree.

T.J. sneaked behind a bush. He tiptoed to the tree. He leaped on the chopper and pedaled furiously down the path.

For about ten minutes T.J. rode around the park. Then he returned to the scene of the crime to see what was happening.

T.J. rode up the path behind the two

trees. The boy was crying. His mother was trying to comfort him.

T.J. rode around in front of the bench and gave the chopper back to the boy. "I found it in the bushes," he said.

The boy couldn't believe his luck. The mother was very grateful. T.J. felt really good and went home.

Dinner

Around six-thirty, T.J.'s mother came home from her office.

"Hi, T.J.," she said. "How was school today?"

"It was all right," said T.J.

"That's good," said his mother. Then she went into the study to talk with T.J.'s father.

After a long time, T.J.'s mother and father went into the kitchen and fixed dinner. When it was ready, they asked T.J. to join them.

Dinner was fish. T.J. didn't like fish, but he ate most of it anyway because he was hungry. T.J.'s parents talked about politics. They didn't talk to T.J. at all.

When dinner was over, T.J. slipped his unused silver knife into a pocket of his jacket. Then he went back to his room and

closed the door. He put the knife into the shopping bag at the back of his closet.

TV

T.J. finished his homework. Then he turned on his portable TV. He watched a program about a good-hearted crook. The crook got away with the money and had a big party at a fancy hotel in Italy.

He watched a movie about a group of thieves digging a tunnel under a bank in Barcelona. The thieves got away with six million dollars and became famous.

Then T.J. went to sleep. He dreamed of getaways down dark, deserted streets. He dreamed of basements full of fancy knives and guns, and policemen chasing after him all over the world.

The Discovery

The next morning the school bus was late. When T.J. got to class, Mr. Peck was already taking attendance.

During math T.J. looked inside his desk under the special pile of papers. The tube of glue was gone! So were Hank's baseball cards and the china dog.

After lunch T.J. checked the desk again. Donald's yellow pad was gone now, and Ted's yo-yo from the other day.

What was going on? Who was doing this to him?

All during recess he went around checking people out. Pamela stopped talking to Georgia Peck when he passed by. Donald wouldn't look at him. Mike was whispering to Hank. How could he tell who it was?

After recess T.J. took another peek in-

side his desk. Nothing else was missing, but on top of the special pile of papers was a note.

The note said: "AFTER SCHOOL TODAY LEAVE JERRY'S POISON RING BY THE GIRLS' BATHROOM DOOR. TIE ALICE'S SCARF AROUND THE FLAGPOLE. LEAVE MARTHA'S PLANE BEHIND SECOND BASE. I'LL GET EVERYTHING RETURNED. THEN I'LL STOP STEALING IF YOU STOP STEALING. THE MYSTERY THIEF."

The Returns

As the afternoon went by, T.J. got more and more nervous. His stomach felt tight, and his hands felt sweaty. In science class he couldn't find his notebook. In art class he spilled the paint.

When school was over, all the kids rushed out the classroom door. T.J. lagged behind, fumbling in his open desk.

"Why, T.J.," said Mr. Peck, "what are you doing still here? You'll miss the bus if you don't hurry."

"Oh," said T.J. "I—uh—I was just looking for something. I won't be more than a minute."

"Okay," said Mr. Peck. "See you in the morning." And he walked out the door.

T.J. was left alone in the classroom. Alone with all those desks full of things. T.J. found

the ring, the scarf, and the plane. He stuffed them in his schoolbag. Then he ran down the hall to the boys' bathroom.

Inside the boys' bathroom it was very quiet. Next door the girls' bathroom seemed very quiet too. T.J. peeked around the boys' bathroom door. No one was coming.

T.J. tiptoed into the hall. He placed Jerry's poison ring beside the girls' bathroom door. The door opened. It was Ms. Cleats, the gym teacher.

"T.J.!" said Ms. Cleats. "What are you doing on the floor?"

"Oh," said T.J., scared to death. "Oh, nothing, Ms. Cleats. I just dropped one of my pencils." And he sprinted to the school yard.

He had a clear path to the flagpole. A few kids were walking out the gate, but no one was nearby. T.J. looked right and left to be sure. He tied Alice's scarf to the base of the flagpole and stood up. Second base was only thirty yards away.

T.J. took Martha's plane out of his schoolbag. He'd always liked it a lot. It had blue
wing tips and a long, sleek body. The school
bus horn was beginning to honk loudly.
Someone was calling his name. T.J. stuffed
the plane back into his bag and ran to the
gate.

So You Thought You Were So Smart

T.J. went straight to his room from the school bus. He checked the ruler in his bedside table and the candy bars under his mattress. He checked the comic book on the shelf and the shopping bag in the closet. Nothing had been disturbed.

T.J. spent the rest of the afternoon in his room. He tried to read but couldn't concentrate. He turned on the TV, but there was nothing he wanted to watch. After dinner he did his homework. Then he went to bed with Martha's plane by his pillow.

The next morning T.J. arrived in class with everyone else. He looked around at the faces. Alice. Mike. Hank. Georgia Peck. No one looked the slightest bit guilty. He looked in his desk. There was another note.

The note said: "**SO YOU THOUGHT YOU**

WERE SO SMART! THIS AFTERNOON YOU
MISS THE SCHOOL BUS. YOU TAKE THE
NUMBER 5 BUS INSTEAD. YOU TAKE IT TO
THE END OF THE LINE. IN THE LITTLE PARK
BESIDE THE HOSPITAL, THERE ARE THREE
BENCHES. LEAVE MARTHA'S PLANE BESIDE
THE FIRST ONE YOU COME TO. THIS IS
YOUR LAST WARNING. THE MYSTERY
THIEF."

Relief

The rest of the school day went by in a blur. T.J. answered a question in math, but he couldn't remember what it was. He did exercises in gym, but he couldn't be sure what kind or how many. When the bell finally rang, he sneaked out the back door and ran to the number 5 bus stop.

The bus took forever to come, but no one saw him waiting. It took forever to reach the end of the line, but no one he knew got on. In the little park beside the hospital, he found the right bench. He placed the plane beside it, and looked back once. Then he ran out of the park and got a bus all the way back to his corner.

The End

When T.J. walked in the door, his father was waiting and looking very upset.

"Hi," said T.J., exhausted.

"Where have you been?" said his father. "The school bus left hours ago. Your mother came home early, and we've both been worried stiff!"

T.J. got very scared. He couldn't admit where he'd been. His father would ask him why. One question would lead to another. He'd be found out.

T.J. took a deep breath. "Oh," he said. "I'm sorry you got worried. I had to stay late at school and help make posters for the play. It took longer than I thought, and I forgot the time and there wasn't any phone around. Mr. Peck gave me a lift home in his car."

His father smiled. "Well, son, I'm glad you're finally getting interested in those things. And how very nice of Mr. Peck. I'll have to give him a call this evening and thank him for us personally."

Later that night, as T.J. got into bed, he heard his father lift the phone to call Mr. Peck. The lie was out.

And More

T.J. sat on his bed looking out the window. It was getting dark. It was getting colder.

Every day for the next three weeks, he had to come right home from school and go to his room. In the evening he could come out for dinner, but that was all. This was only the third day, and already there were no more comic books to read, no more candy bars under the mattress, and no more TV that was any fun. What a price to pay for lying to your father.

He opened his book of bad men. Waxed mustaches smirked up at him. He leaned back on his bed. He looked up at the ceiling.

A moment later he heard his father's footsteps. They stopped outside his door. "Late mail," his father said. An envelope was slipped under the door. The footsteps trailed away.

T.J. rushed to pick up the envelope. Sure enough, it was addressed to him. The handwriting looked vaguely familiar. He tore open the seal and pulled out the note.

The note said: "**HEY, MAN! CONGRATU-LATIONS! I HEAR YOU'VE BECOME AS GOOD A LIAR AS YOU WERE A THIEF. TUT, TUT. BETTER LUCK NEXT TIME. GEORGIA PECK.**"